# LOVE & LIFE

# Douglas A. Lawton

LIVITY BOOKS

# LOVE AND LIFE

**ISBN  978-1-941632-01-7**  (Paper)


**Published by**

Livity Books

West Palm Beach, FL 33416

# Table of Contents

## Looking For Something

Everybody's looking for something:
Something unique to call their own;
Something to excite and ignite;
Something to take them to the highest height;
Something deep and enduring;
Something unpredictable, worth exploring;
Something steady, worth pursuing;
Something unbelievably real;
Something mind-boggling surreal;
Something with meaning you can feel;
Something exploding, you can't conceal;
Everybody's looking for something.

### Yearning

What it is?
Who it is?
Sometimes not known.
Yet there is yearning,
Desiring,
Longing.
Like matters arising,
Evolving.
When you see it,
Your heart skips a beat.
When you hear it,
It's like music, oh, so sweet.
Despite complexity,
This is your reality.
As paths intersect,
You connect.
Desire meeting opportunity,
Producing the surreal.
Something resonating within,
Making you want to dance or sing.

## Love Is What It Is

This spell-binding attraction,
Unprecedented adoration,
Causing feelings of elation.

This evolving situation,
Unsettling emotion,
Resulting in destabilization.

This overwhelming reaction,
Needing satisfaction,
A source of distraction.

This sense of connection,
Needing affirmation,
Desiring expression.

This strong affection.
This feeling of gratification.
Love is what it is.

## Find Someone...Be That One

Find someone able and willing to complement you,
 Not someone incompatible and in contest with you.
Find someone able and willing to communicate,
 Not someone argumentative, always wanting a debate.
Find someone with a brain, wise and discerning,
 Not someone like a parrot obtuse and regurgitating.
Find someone willing to involve you,
 Not someone who wants to dictate or control you.
Find someone able and willing to be creative with you,
 Not someone wanting to recreate or convert you.
Find someone uplifting and energizing,
 Not someone berating and sermonizing.
Find someone able and willing to accept you,
 Not someone who wants to change you.
Find someone willing to relate as an adult,
 Not someone who wants to mother or father you.
Find someone willing to help you grow,
 Not someone who wants to inhibit you.
Find someone who encourages and strengthens you,
 Not someone who discourages and weakens you.
Find someone willing and able to support you,
 Not someone who only wants to lean on you.
Find someone who is self-assured,
 Not someone lacking in confidence or insecure.
Find someone with whom you can be intimate,
 Not someone who merely wants to copulate.
Find someone contented and healthy,
 Not someone needing you to be happy and wealthy.
Find someone able and willing to appreciate you,
 Not someone who takes you for granted.
Find someone with integrity,
 Not someone divided and clothed in uncertainty.

Find someone who makes you laugh,
  Not someone who is a plaintive bore.
Find someone who can laugh at self,
  Not someone who takes him/herself too seriously.
Find someone adventurous and spontaneous,
  Not someone too programmed and predictable.
Find someone competent and teachable,
  Not someone ignorant and impeachable.
Find someone empathetic and forgiving,
  Not someone malicious and vindictive.
Find someone willing to be corrected,
  Not someone egoistic and bigoted.
Find someone sedate and patient,
  Not someone anxious to join the rat race.
Find someone with whom you can plan,
  Not a disorganized and disconcerting drifter.
Find someone who knows how to be discreet,
  Not someone talkative and secrets repeat.
Find someone truly spiritual and knows how to pray,
  Not a hypocrite or religious fanatic.
Find someone deep and able to discuss ideas,
  Not someone petty and engrossed in trivia.
Find someone with whom you can tango,
  Not someone with whom you're obliged to tangle.
Find someone genuine, true to the core,
  Not someone artificial who will not endure.
Find someone you can rely on,
  Not someone constantly moving on.
Find someone with whom you can confide,
  Not someone, some things you're forced to hide.
Find someone willing and able to work with you,
  Not someone who just wants to work you.
Find someone...be that one.

### Falling In Love

Do not fall in love with things;
    Fall in love with people.
Things may improve your status;
    It takes people to improve your standing.
Things may guarantee you an income;
    It takes people to sustain you when there's none.
Things may make you better-off;
    It takes people to make you well.
Things may enhance your lifestyle.
    It takes people to enhance your life.
Things may help you negotiate;
    It takes people to reciprocate.
Things may get you in the inner circle;
    It takes people to get you around it.
Things may make you comfortable;
    It takes people to bring you comfort.
Things may get you sex;
    It takes people to give you love.
Things may bring you glory;
    It takes people to bring God's story.
Do not fall in love with things;
    Fall in love with people.

## Money Can't Buy Love

There are many things money can buy.
It's a powerful tool, I'll tell you why.
Money can buy friends and influence.
It may purchase property and opulence.
But money can't buy love that's sincere;
For there's nothing to leverage or compare.
Buying love may put you in a deep pit.
If there's no money, your lover may quit.
Further, buying love is like paying rent.
Soon you'll wonder where the money went.
Stop paying and you'll be evicted.
Play the fool and you'll be convicted.
Yet money is good – get plenty of it.
Without money, many things you'll forfeit.
You can use money in expression of your love,
And do great things to honor the Father above.
Yet if you live for money, you'll be disappointed,
For money is just a tool for use as appointed.
"The fool and his money will soon depart."
So guard your money and guard your heart.
Money can consume you beyond measure.
And may be the source of much displeasure.

## What Is Love?

It is a concept and condition;
A prognosis and recommendation.
It is the virtue most admired;
The life that is most desired.

Love has an empowering quality.
It has an enduring reality.
Love is freedom undefined.
It is passion unrefined.

Love empowers the soul.
It is the gift that makes you whole.
Love enables health.
It is the source of true wealth.

Love liberates the spirit;
It enables grace and grit.
Love fires the imagination.
It's the source of all creation.

Love makes you strong.
It makes you right, not wrong.
Love is giving and receiving.
And love keeps you believing.

| LOVE IS NOT | LOVE IS |
|---|---|
| Love is not insensitive. | Love is caring and attending. |
| Love is not excluding. | Love is including. |
| Love is not patronizing. | Love is accommodating. |
| Love is not envious. | Love is well-meaning. |
| Love is not proud. | Love is humble. |
| Love is not discouraging. | Love is encouraging. |
| Love is not vindictive. | Love is helpful and forgiving. |
| Love is not devaluing. | Love is valuing and uplifting. |
| Love is not unfaithful. | Love is loyal. |
| Love is not disrespectful. | Love is respectful. |
| Love is not evil and mean. | Love is good and kind. |
| Love is not condemning. | Love is redeeming. |
| Love is not ungrateful. | Love is appreciative. |
| Love is not selfish. | Love is considerate. |
| Love is not hypocritical. | Love is sincere and genuine. |
| Love is not easily angered. | Love is composed and patient. |
| Love is not contentious. | Love is peaceful. |
| Love is not careless. | Love is careful and protective. |
| Love is not demanding. | Love is respectfully assertive. |
| Love is not suspicious. | Love is trusting. |
| Love is not quitting. | Love is persevering. |
| Love is not hypercritical. | Love is fair and constructive. |
| Love is not pessimistic. | Love is optimistic. |
| Love is not paralyzing. | Love is empowering. |

## Attitudes of Love

Be admirable.

Be appreciative.

Be affirming.

Be caring.

Be considerate.

Be compassionate.

Be confidential.

Be content.

Be composed.

Be courageous.

Be creative.

Be encouraging.

Be empowering.

Be fair.

Be forgiving

Be generous.

Be happy

Be helpful

Be humble.

Be honest

Be intelligent.

Be jovial.

Be kind.

Be loyal.

Be optimistic.

Be peaceful.

Be passionate.

Be pleasant

Be pure.

Be protective.

Be persevering.

Be respectful.

Be sincere.

Be trustful.

Be truthful.

Be thankful.

Be merciful

Be wise.

## False Caad

Mi ask har fi a date,
She snub mi, meking mi ego deflate.
Di gal looking so nice an sweet
Busup mi hart, mi head heng in defeat.
Cole as ice, she put mi ina mi place,
Dissing I an I, memba of di human race.
Next time mi si har she was hitching a ride,
So mi stap an pick har up ina mi Escalide.
Maasah, di gal start fi flirt wid mi,
Telling mi how she luv pickney.
She tell mi how mi look strong an cute
An dat she woulda luv fi gi mi a yute.
Mi ask har if she have house an lan.
She seh no, but she can mek mi a happy man.
Imagine, di same gal who dissed mi before,
A mek mi out fi be a man she could adore.
She was certainly having quite a dream,
Tinking a woulda fall fi panty scheme.
Mi jus hurry up an drap har at har yaad,
Tell har gweh far mi caan win wid false caad.

## Betrayed

You said you loved me,
And I believed it.
But loving him?
I could not conceive it.
Being my very best friend,
My heart you surely rend.
What happened?
How did it come to this?
Betrayed by you?
Betrayed by him?
This is a nightmare!
How could I not see
You were only acting for me?
You played me to get close;
He was the man, and I the ghost.
Must have been trying too hard,
Not to sense there was discord.
Should have taken my cue.
Really wasn't getting my due.
There were many a doubt,
But I reasoned them out.
At times I did sense treason,
Yet could not see the reason.
It's okay; I am over you now.
Life always proceeds somehow.

## Taking Care of Uncle

I knew he was dear to you,
Cause you took care of Uncle.
At least you prepared his breakfast.
What else you did?
...I wasn't sure,
But you took care of Uncle.
I wondered if it was for the big house:
You had a special thing!
But he was Uncle.
Probably needed security,
A father-figure, maybe.
So you took care of Uncle.
Weeks turned to months
And months to years:
You were taking care of Uncle.
His wife had died;
Children scattered wide.
So you took care of Uncle.
What a faithful girl!
How admirable!
But it was Uncle who was taking care of you.
You've been seeing him right under my nose.
He was knocking you up
And you filled his cup.
Willingly engaging in the ritual,
Although claiming to be spiritual.
I wondered where your morals went:
All those years together we had spent.
His children displeased, threw you out,
Surprised you were taking care of Uncle.

## This Juggling Act

The heart must rule the head, 'tis said.
Yet head ruling heart leaves emotions dead.
When heart rules, there're aches and pain,
A lot of turmoil and sometimes no gain.
Oh baby, it is hard to do this juggling act.
This needs skills I'm not sure I have got.
The ball has been coming so fast,
Making me wonder if this can last.
I'm not good at jumping all this rope.
I really do not know that I can cope.
Blood flowing head to toe,
Mind going to and fro.
Body going into overdrive,
Mouth wanting to *salavive*.
Emotions leaving me undone,
Causing much longing for you to come,
Wanting earnestly to satisfy desire,
Hoping together we can calm the fire.

## Euphoria

Curves in perfect symmetry.
Mesmerizing.
My heart and soul she shook.
Captivating.
I could only surrender.
Yielding.
Rhythmic movements.
Exhilarating.
Articulating with alacrity.
Pleasing.
Conferring bliss.
Adoring.
Exuding love.
Exploding.
Exulting in ecstasy.
Dying.
Reviving again.
Lavishing.
Coming again.
Exhausting.
In a moment,
Vanishing!
Leaving me breathless.
Longing.
She was there.
I could see her sparkling eyes
Filling my gaping heart with love.
But I must sleep on
To maintain my illusion.

### Conflicted

So sorry that you want to say "goodbye:"
There is turmoil and a sigh;
Encumbered by the burden you bear.
It feels like this because you care.
Caring is what makes you who you are:
My precious gem, my shining star.
Whatever you decide, I am with you still.
Loving you is to respect your will.
Do what you must;
I will have to adjust.
Loving you is to set you free,
To have what you deserve and desire to be.

## Strutting Your Stuff

Strutting what seems your stuff.
Carrying it as if you're a prof.
Everything's screaming,
I know I'm not dreaming.
What's behind is printing out.
What's in front is giving a shout.
The fluff, amazingly spread,
Comes crashing in my head.
Everything's on display,
Causing much dismay.
It's a riddle - perhaps not!
Clearly you think you're hot.
Yet I can't keep off my eyes.
Am forced to scrutinize.
Though at times confusing,
You are certainly amusing.
Mission is accomplished,
Now I'm an accomplice.
Indeed, you've won the day,
Causing me to watch and pray.

## Don't Let Me Go

Don't let me go.
Don't let me go.
I want to be with you;
If only you knew.
Keep me in your arms.
Silence all alarms.
Never let me go.

Don't let me go.
Don't let me go.
Even if I stray,
I'll soon find my way.
Let me see your face
And feel your embrace.
Never let me go.

Don't let me go.
Don't let me go.
You're the only one I know,
And I want to keep it so.
My desire is only for you.
Let us see it through.
Never let me go.

## Crazy Love

He's connected to Sue for her pretty looks,
And to Meghan for her talk on books.
He said he needed intellectual stimulation.
Plus Meghan was better at communication.
With Meghan, he could talk about anything.
With Sue, it was small talk and gossiping.
Sue was a cantankerous, implacable shrew.
So with her he did not know what to do.
Sue was the spouse giving him crazy sex.
Meghan was the friend keeping him in context.
Sue stayed in order to improve her situation.
He kept her for sex and social gratification.
Sue had the right color and social class,
Meghan was black and of a lower caste.
Paul was in love with Sue's body,
But loved Meghan for camaraderie.
He claimed there is no complete package,
That everyone has their own wattage.
So Meghan was the brain supporting,
But Sue was the one wearing the ring.

## Longing

I long
To touch you,
To sense you,
To smell you,
To look at you,
To see you smile,
To humor you,
To watch you play,
To tease you,
To see you sigh,
To enjoy you,
To look into your eyes,
To hear your voice,
And to hear you say,
"I love you."

## Mirror, Mirror

Mirror,
Mirror.
Vivid imagination.
Surreal expectation.
Hot indeed, not cold.
Bought and sold.
Heart-pounding vibration.
Overwhelming admiration.
Desire defeating suppression.
Aspiration diminishing opposition.
Profound ideation,
Eclipsed by consummation.
Borders lifted.
Boundaries crossed.
Conflicted.
Convicted.
Falling short,
Yet standing tall.
Emotions intense –
A consuming fire.
Loving and longing.
A sense of belonging.
Knowing me
Is knowing you.
Mirror,
Mirror.

### Heart of Stone

Wanna break through your heart of stone,
Heart of stone.
You're so used to being alone,
Being alone.
Baby I wanna get close to you,
Close to you.
I wanna break through your heart of stone.

Wanna break through your heart of stone,
Heart of stone.
I just can't leave you alone,
Leave you alone.
Baby I wanna come home to you,
Home to you.
I wanna break through your heart of stone.

Wanna break through your heart of stone,
Heart of stone.
Baby I need to break through to you,
Through to you.
I just can't leave you alone,
Leave you alone.
Baby I wanna come home to you,
Home to you.
I wanna break through your heart of stone.

## Journeying On

On the road.
On the road.
Carrying my heavy load,
Fearing I might implode.
Unpleasant stuff,
Making life rough.
I'm journeying on.

On the road.
On the road.
Unfulfilled dreams.
Occasional screams,
And sighs between.
No one on whom to lean.
I'm journey on.

On the road.
On the road.
Craving a brand new scene,
Somewhere quiet and serene,
A special sweet treat,
With no one to compete.
I'm journey on.

On the road.
On the road.
Unpleasant sounds abounding,
People rude and overbearing.
Cast down but not forsaken.
Tomorrow is not yet taken.
I'm journeying on.

On the road.
On the road.
I shall not give in.
There's power within.
This is not the final dance.
There's still another chance.
I'm journeying on.

On the road,
On the road.
I've found my queen.
An angel pure and clean.
Beauty indescribably deep.
Someone whom I'll keep.
We're journeying on.

## Messing Up My Mind

You again.
You again.
Messing up my mind.
It's you again.

Just one hit.
Now always wanting it.
Messing up my mind.
It's you again.

Breaking.
Diminishing.
Messing up my mind.
It's you again.

Consuming.
Controlling.
Messing up my mind.
It's you again.

Hilarity.
Perplexity.
Messing up my mind.
It's you again.

Taking.
There's no escaping.
Messing up my mind.
It's you again.

Taking me high.
Bringing me low.
Messing up my mind.
It's you again.

You again.
You again.
Messing up my mind.
It's you again.

## All I Want Is You

My history with you
Is indeed a mystery.
All of you,
All of me,
In sync.
In so short a time
We intertwined,
Leaving me pondering,
How could this be?
Your voice, captivating.
Your body, alluring.
Your mind, inspiring.
Titillating mind and body,
You shook my soul,
Making me whole.
Finally complementarity
Fusing in solidarity.
It's a beautiful dance,
A sweet romance.
It's a fantasy!
Reading like fiction.
Seems too good to be true;
Yet all that I want is you.

## Other Works by the Author

Spiritual Intelligence: A Christian Perspective

Caribbean Crime and Violence

Marriage Under Siege

The Marriage Relationship

Before Marriage: A Primer

The Compatibility Questionnaire

Positive Vibrations

Value Vibes (Workbooks 1-6)

We Can (Workbooks 1-6)

The Mentee's Journal

Meet Mr. Bigot

The Supremacists' Conspiracy

Contending With Bigotry

My Prayer: Petitions For The Spiritual Mind

www.ingramcontent.com/pod-product-compliance
Lightning Source LLC
Chambersburg PA
CBHW072048170626
46811CB00008B/3210

* 9 7 8 1 9 4 1 6 3 2 0 1 7 *